Wallace & Gromit ™

AND THE LOST SLIPPER

Text by **Tristan Davies**

Drawings by **Nick Newman**

Hodder & Stoughton

Lettering by Garry Gilbert

First published in Great Britain in 1997
by Hodder & Stoughton
A division of Hodder Headline PLC

10 9 8 7 6 5 4 3 2 1

A CIP catalogue record for this title is available from the British Library.

ISBN 0 8417 2026 6
Printed in Belgium by Proost International Book Production

Published in the United States
Distribooks Inc.
8120 N. Ridgeway
SKOKIE, IL. 60076
Tel. (847) 676-1596
Toll free Fax (888) 266-5713

Aardman animations

As the stars of any animated film would tell you if they could, being an animated character can be very frustrating. You spend long periods of time moving very, very slowly, millimetre by millimetre, for the cameras. And then in between films you spend long periods of time not moving at all while resting on the shelf in your creator's studio.

Wallace and Gromit, with their huge appetite for life and high-protein dairy products, refused to take all this lying down lying down. They cried out, albeit completely silently, to be let loose in exciting new cheesy adventures. And because both characters have legs, as they say – four in Gromit's case, even though he often only walks on two of them – I was delighted to allow the pair to stretch them across the printed page.

I do hope you enjoy *The Lost Slipper* and *The Curse of the Ramsbottoms*, the first two stories in a series of new comic strip adventures for Wallace and Gromit, as much as they enjoyed not having to gather dust resting up on that shelf in the Aardman studio.

Nick Park

Aardman Animations Ltd Directors: Peter Lord, David Sproxton and Nick Park
Gas Ferry Road Bristol BS1 6UN England
Tel: 0117 984 8485 Fax: 0117 984 8486 http://www.aardman.com
Registered Office Address as above Registered in England and Wales Registration number: 2050843
VAT Registration number: GB 609 3011 72

DRAMATIS PERSONAE
(Which according to Gromit's written translation, is Latin for 'whom you are about to receive')

WALLACE
Inventor, handyman, cheese-fancier – and for the purposes of this story, a man who has lost his slipper but not his marbles.

GROMIT
Constant companion, housekeeper and dog – Gromit does all the doggy things you'd expect: he sits, he stays, he does algebra in his head while speed-knitting.

WILLIAM THE CONQUEROR
A conqueror from Normandy, called William, whose subjugation of the Anglo-Saxon people is a piece of cake compared to all the dreadful meals he is forced to eat in England.

BARON WALLAIS DE WALLAIS
Inventor, handyman and convicted coiffeur, this Norman ancestor was years ahead of his time when he tunnelled out of a French prison cell and under the Channel to England. Sadly, history only remembers him for his use of small furry animals with sharp teeth while trying to perfect a do-it-yourself medieval pudding basin haircutting system. It did not catch on.

UG-WALLACE
Inventor, handyman and non-shaver, this even more distant forebear held the world land speed rollerblading record (uncontested) in One Million Years B.C. A celebrated wit and conversationalist – if your idea of a good conversation involves going 'Ug-ug-ug' a lot.

WALLACE'S GREAT-GREAT-GREAT NEPHEW
Inventor, handyman and hopping mad eco-warrior, Great-Great-Great Uncle Wallace's future relative has a bee in his baseball cap about families who drive more than one pair of clogs.

THE PHARAOHS
Ancient Egyptians, sandal-wearers and confirmed cat-lovers, there's not much to say about Queen Neferti-tea-for-two-tu-tankha-etc. – except that it's much simpler just to call them Mr and Mrs Pharaoh.

I SAY, GROMIT. HAVE YOU SEEN MY OTHER CARPET SLIPPER, PERCHANCE?

I HAVEN'T SEEN IT SINCE THE 11.06 DELIVERED THE MAIL...

...AND IT'S NOT IN THE FRIDGE WHERE I USUALLY KEEP IT FOR THAT EXTRA DEGREE OF SUMMER-FRESH COOLNESS.

PERHAPS IT WAS 'ACCIDENTALLY MISLAID' BY A CERTAIN CANINE COMPANION. I MUST GET TO THE BOTTOM OF THIS.

A ROMAN VILLA... BURIED TREASURE... AND LOTS OF OIL! BUT NO COMFY CARPET SLIPPER, HMM. I'LL HAVE TO FIND A REPLACEMENT, ANY IDEAS, GROMIT?

CANINESTEIN'S THEORY OF RELATIVITY

BUILDING AN UN-WEAROUTABLE SUBSTITUTE WILL BE AN ENVIRON-MENTALLY-SENSITIVE OPERATION...

...WHICH IS WHY WE'LL NEED ALL THE RIVETS AND RECYCLED BAKED BEAN CANS WE CAN FIND...

DOGCATCHER IN THE RYE

BEAN

HAS-BEAN CANS

...NOT TO MENTION A GENEROUS SUPPLY OF DANGEROUS TOOLS AND CHEESY NIBBLES.

THERE YOU ARE, GROMIT. THE LONGLIFE INDOOR CARPET CLOG/ SENSIBLE HOUSEHOLD BROGUE WITH REINFORCED EVERYTHING.

OBVIOUSLY IT NEEDS A BIT OF WEARING IN.

I'VE HEARD OF TRENCH FOOT, BUT THIS IS RIDICULOUS. NOW WE'VE *GOT* TO FIND MY SLIPPER. IF ONLY WE COULD TURN BACK THE CLOCK...

A BRIEF HISTORY OF TIME STEPHEN BARKING

1

CRIKEY. PREPARE TO REPEL BURROWERS, GROMIT.

CRUMBLING COURGETTES!

PIGGADIGGADIGGA!

'ER-RACK!

BONJOUR TOUT LE MONDE! FREEDOM AT LAST FROM MY FRENCH PRISON CELL! OÙ AM I EXACTLY?

UNDERGROUND MAP
YE NORMAN LINE

IN AN **ENGLISH** PRISON CELL, CHUCK.

SACRÉ-DRAT! IT SEEMS I'VE INVENTED SOME KIND OF FIXED LINK SHUTTLE FROM MAINLAND EUROPE WITH SERVICES ON THE MILLENNIUM. NOBODY'S EVER GOING TO WANT THAT.

PERMIT-NOUS TO INTRODUCE OURSELVES. BARON WALLAIS DE WALLAIS, INVENTOR EXTRAORDINAIRE, AND MY TRUSTY HOUND, GROMIT-LE-CHIEN.

BY 'ECK YOU LOOK FAMILIAR...

I KNOW! YOU'RE ONE THERMAL CHAIN-MAIL SOCK SHORT OF A MATCHING PAIR! QUEL COINCIDENCE!

WE'RE ON THE TRAIL OF AN EVIL MEDIEVAL TIME-TRAVELLING FOOTWEAR THIEF AND NO MISTAKE!

LATER THAT DAY...

...AND I WAS JAILED FOR MY MOST INFLUENTIAL INVENTION YET...

...THE MEDIEVAL PUDDING BASIN HAIRCUTTER WITH SELF-TRIMMING STOAT-OF-THE-ART FRINGE SYSTEM.

THE CHOICE OF STYLES WAS SO POPULAR THEY PUT ME IN PRISON FOR MY OWN SAFETY.

THAT'S ALL VERY WELL, BUT WITH FOUR TO A CELL WE'LL HAVE TO START STRETCHING OUR RATIONS.

S·T·R·E·T·C·H

OH YES. I'VE GOT HIM WELL TRAINED.

VERY INTERESTING -- BUT WE FRENCH WILL NEVER SWALLOW IT. I, HOWEVER, KNOW JUST WHAT TO DO WITH YOUR SO-CALLED **ENGLISH** 'FRENCH STICK'.........

GULP!

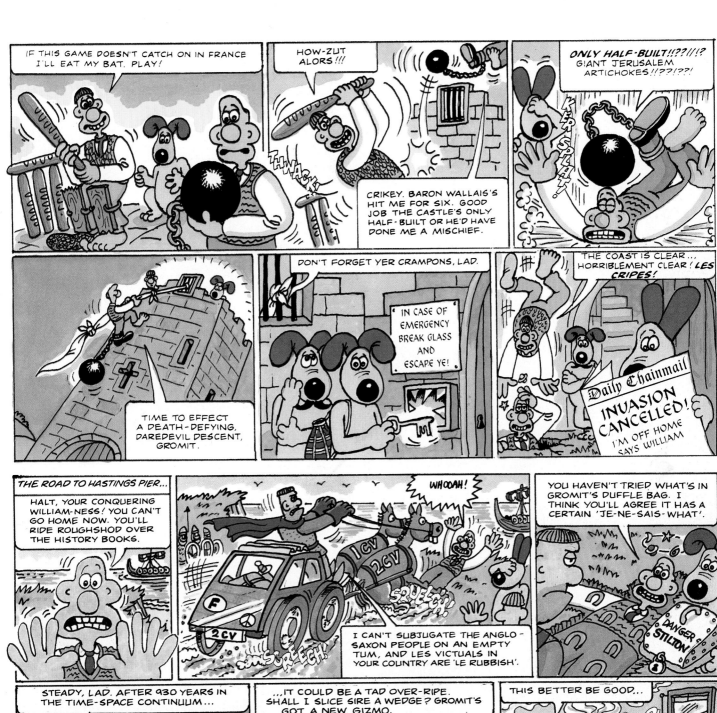

SUFFERING SAXONS! YOUR STILTON REALLY IS *MAGNIFIQUE*. CAN I HAVE THE RECIPE?

YOU CAN IF I CAN HAVE MY TIME MACHINE BACK.

THANKS TO YOUR CHEESY ENGLISH NIBBLES, WE HUNGRY FRENCH SHALL CONTINUE OUR INVASION. BUT FIRST WE WILL CELEBRATE THE HISTORIC BIRTH OF THE ECU -- THE EUROPEAN CHEESY UNIT.

CHEESE MADE SIMPLE

YE FIRST EVER MEDIEVAL CHEESE 'N' WINE PARTY

AS I SAID, I'VE GOT HIM WELL TRAINED.

LE CHIT. LE CHATTER.

ENCORE, MONSIEUR WALLY. HIC! SHOW US YOUR SHAKE-IT-ALL-ABOUT SO-CALLED 'OKEY-COKEY.'

ALTOGETHER NOW: YOU STICK YER LEFT LEG IN, YOU STICK YER-

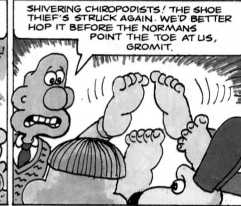

SHIVERING CHIROPODISTS! THE SHOE THIEF'S STRUCK AGAIN. WE'D BETTER HOP IT BEFORE THE NORMANS POINT THE TOE AT US, GROMIT.

STOPPEZ-THEM -- AND SEARCH THEIR GRANDFATHER'S CLOCK -- HE MIGHT BE IN ON IT, TOO.

NOW, TELL ME WHICH ONE FILCHED OUR NORMAN FOOTWEAR OR FACE THE HORROR OF...

DUNGEON SWEET DUNGEON

TRIAL BY CHEESE!!!...IN WHICH YOUR OWN EXQUISITE STILTON MAY BE TAKEN DOWN AND USED AGAINST YOU...,

...WAFTED JUST TANTALISING EURO-INCHES FROM YOUR NOSE UNTIL YOU TALK -- OR DIE OF DESIRE.

GULP!

HOURS OF CHEESY TORMENT LATER...

YOUR TORTURINGNESS. I CAN'T SAY 'WHO FILCHED YOUR FOT SOLDIERS' FEETWEAR'. I DON'T KNOW.

THEN I'LL BE BACK TOMORROW -- WITH A DOUBLE HELPING OF CHEESE - AND *CRACKERS!!*

DEMENTED DAIRY FARMERS! MY NOSE'LL NEVER TAKE IT!

FEAR NOT, WALLACE. I HAVE UN PLAN. BUT FIRST YOU NEED A NEW HAIRCUT...

I ALWAYS HAD FAITH IN YOUR MEDIEVAL PUDDING BASIN HAIRCUTTER WITH SELF-TRIMMING STOAT-OF-THE ART FRINGE SYSTEM.

AND AT LAST WE'VE FOUND A USE FOR MY FIXED LINK SHUTTLE TO MAINLAND EUROPE.

GOOD NEWS - I'VE TUNNELED DOWN TO MY TUNNEL! NEXT STOP - LIBERTÉ!

YOU'D BETTER BORROW A LONGLIFE CARPET CLOG 'TIL WE CATCH THE SHOE THIEF. BON VOYAGE, CHUCK!

AUF WIEDERSEHEN PET - AND DON'T FORGET LE TUNNEL IS ONLY A PROTOTYPE.

CRIKEY - WHO KNOWS WHERE WE'LL END UP. YOUR TURN TO MAP-READ GROMIT, METHINKS.

THEY'RE RIGHT, LAD. THE TUNNEL IS A LOT QUICKER THAN THE---

BOOOAAAAAAT!!!

WHEEE!

ACCELERATING CELERY STICKS! I CAN'T HOLD HER. WE'RE GOING TO JUMP THE LIIIIGHTS!

YIKES. WE'RE MOVING SO FAST WE'RE BEGINNING TO DEMA--

SCRREEE

--TERIALISE ... COLOSSAL CARNIVORES! WHATEVER TIME IT IS THEY CERTAINLY CATER FOR DOGS.

EEECH!

ONE MILLION YEARS BEFORE CHEESE! OH NO! I GET THE INFINITE DEPRESSION IT ISN'T CHEDDAR THEY PUT ON THEIR CRACKERS. HELP!

1 MILLION B.C.

KER'THUD!

FINDING MY SLIPPER NOW IS GOING TO BE A MAMMOTH, ER, TUSK. WE'D BETTER SET UP OUR BASE CAMP.

MAKE YOURSELF USEFUL WHILE I ERECT THE DORMOVANCAMPMOBILETENTETTE WITH ENSUITE FACILITIES.

FER-LAP!

THIS IS NO TIME TO BURY BONES, LAD.

MIND YOU HE IS ONLY A DOG, I SUPPOSE.

WELL DONE, GROMIT. VERY 'BONES & GARDENS'. WE'LL HAVE A CAMP-WARMING WITH THE LAST OF OUR CHEDDAR.

MEN DOGS

BEWARE OF THE MAN

HUNGRY HUMANOIDS! THE AROMA OF MELTING CHEESE HAS ATTRACTED COMPANY. D'YOU THINK HE'S HAD HIS TEA?

UG!

UG UG UG. UG UG UG. OG!

HE'S AFTER OUR TUCK. HE'S PROBABLY NEVER SEEN A FLAME-GRILLED CHEESE TOASTIE BEFORE.

UG UG UG. UG UG UG. OG!

NOW DON'T TRY ANY MONKEY BUSINESS WITH ME, MATE, OR YOU'LL BE HEARING FROM MY D-OG.

YOU'D BETTER LOOK OUT OR YOU'LL BURN YOUR FINGERS IN THE--

?

O-O-O-O-O-O...

...A-A-A-A-A-A-G-H-H!!

THAT'S THE TROUBLE WITH BONE AGE MAN; TOTALLY BONE-HEADED ABOUT NEW TECHNOLOGY.

D-OG. D-OG. D-OG.

GROMIT'S A D-OG ALL RIGHT. AND NOW IF YOU'RE FEELING BETTER YOU CAN HELP HIM FIND MY SLIPPER.

READING HIS BODY LANGUAGE, I'LL TAKE THAT AS AN 'UG'.

WEEKS OF RECUPERATION LATER...

THESE EARLY ROLLERBLADES ARE LETHAL. I MUST INVENT A MEANS OF SLOWING THEM DOWN.

A NAVIGATIONAL, GRAVITATIONAL, OVERSHOOT PARACHUTE WOULD BE...

... USELESS IF THERE WERE A FOLLOWING WIND.

AND A PAIR OF IMMOBILISING AND STABILISING...

... ANCHORS ARE NOT THE WAY.

IF ONLY I COULD CUT SOME CORNERS WITH MY RESEARCH...

CUT SOME CORNERS!! EUREKA!!

I'LL REINVENT THE WHEEL -- AND MAKE IT AN OCTO-, HEDRA-, POLYUNSATURATED-, ER, NOT-QUITE-ROUND-ONE.

IF THAT DOESN'T SLOW 'EM DOWN FOR A MILLENNIUM, NOTHING WILL.

MAKE UP A SET OF THESE, CHUCK, AND HIGH-SPEED ROLLERBLADE CRASHES WILL BE A THING OF THE FUTURE...

UG?

... ASK YER CHUM TO EXPLAIN. HE LOOKS THE INTELLECTUAL TYPE...

...MIND YOU, HE APPEARS TO BE BARKING UP THE WRONG TREE...

... CRACKPOT CANINES! NOW HE'S MISSING THE POINT COMPLETELY...

...HE'S NOT MAKING MY REVOLUTIONARY NO-REVOLUTIONS PER SECOND, GO-SLOWER ROLLERBLADE WHEEL...

... HE'S JUST A DOG WHO'S GOT THE WRONG END OF THE STICK. BARK SOME SENSE INTO HIM, GROMIT. GO ON, LAD!

THEY'LL NEVER RE-INVENT THE WHEEL LYING DOWN ON THE JOB LIKE THAT...

BDOING-!!

STILL, THEY PROVE ONE THING: JAW-JAW IS JUST AS GOOD AS SAW-SAW.

SIX MONTHS...

R-RUMBLE!

UG!

...AND SEVEN SLIPPED DISCS LATER...

T-UG!

GRAND -UG- OPENING

AT LAST! MY NOT-QUITE ROUND WHEEL SHOULD MAKE A MAJOR CONTRIBUTION TO ROAD SAFETY, AND...

STONE THE HENGES!

UG UG' LIVING HERITAGE AND INTERESTING OLD ROCKS VISITOR CENTRE! UG.

ER, VERY INTERESTING, I'M SURE - BUT WHAT EXACTLY IS IT *FOR*, WHEN IT'S AT HOME?

BUT GROMIT HAS OTHER PLANS!

ROLLERBLADING RASPBERRIES!

SPECTATORS' CAR PARK

BY 'ECK, OLD FRIEND,...

...YOU NEVER PUT ON A SHOW...

...AS GOOD AS THIS...

...AT OBEDIENCE CLASSES!

MORE!

5·9

5·9

6·0

UG·WOOF!

5·7

5·9

UG·CORE!

BRAVO, LAD. BRAVO. I WAS SO TAKEN BY YOUR DISPLAY I COMPLETELY FAILED TO NOTICE...

...THAT--*ROLLICKING ROLLERBLADES!!!* THAT SHOE THIEF'S STRUCK AGAIN. AND THIS TIME HE'S LEFT A CLUE...

SPECTATORS' CAR PARK

CHEESE

DEFINITELY WENSLEYDALE! THE SHOE THIEF'S A CHEESE LOVER, ALL RIGHT.

GET AFTER HIM, GROMIT, BEFORE THE TRAIL GOES COLD.

AND WRAP UP WARM-- IT LOOKS LIKE ...

...SNOW!!

NOW THAT'S WHAT I CALL A COMPLETE WHITE-OUT

THE BLIZZARD EVENTUALLY STOPS BUT THE TRAIL IS OBSCURED. GROMIT HEADS HOME, HIS TAIL BETWEEN HIS LEGS ...

... AND HIS MASTER IN A SOLID PICKLE...

W-WATCH OUT G-GROMIT THE ICE AGE C-C-COMETH

BY NIGHTFALL, GROMIT HAS DEVISED A BRILLIANT CANINE CONCEPT...

HEAVE!

SLIIIDE!

... AND AS DAWN DAWNS...

BRRRING!

ZZZZ

... ON THE LONGEST DAY...

FIZZZZ!

DELIRIOUS DRUIDS, GROMIT! A SOLAR-POWERED LASER-LAUNCHING OXY-ACETYLENE, ER, SHAVING MIRROR THAT ONLY WORKS ON MIDSUMMER'S DAY! I KNEW THOSE STONES HAD A PURPOSE.

BUT LET'S GET AFTER THE SHOE THIEF. MY FOOT FEELS, WELL, LIKE A BLOCK OF ICE.

WE'LL LEAVE OUR FROZEN FRIENDS SOME OF OUR LONGLIFE CARPET CLOGS IN CASE GLOBAL WARMING STARTS BEFORE WE GET THEIR FOOTWEAR BACK.

LATER...

MUSH! MUSH! *M-U-S-H!* C'MON LAD. YOU'LL HAVE TO PULL FASTER...

STRAIN! HEAVE! PANT!

... ALL THIS SHOUTING'S MAKING MY VOICE GO HUSKY!

CRACKERS

WELL DONE, LAD. ANOTHER CLUE. THAT SHOE THIEF TAKES THE BISCUIT, ALL RIGHT.

CRESTA RUN-UG-UG

BETTER GET AFTER HIM, TALLY HO! FOLLOW THAT, ER, CREAM CRACKER!

WHOOOOSH!

WE'RE ON THE RIGHT TRACK ALL RIGHT. THERE'S KING HAROLD'S STOLEN BATTLE SANDAL...

...PLUS ALL HIS BANDAGES AND GIANT TINS OF CAT FOOD.

HIS BANDAGES AND GIANT TINS OF CAT FOOD!!! HELP!!!! WE MUST BE MALFUNCTIONING.

CRASH! BUMP! KER-THUMP!

MUMMIFIED MARROWS, GROMIT!!!!

WE'RE UP A PYRAMID, ALL RIGHT, AND WE HAVEN'T GOT A PADDLE TO STAND ON.

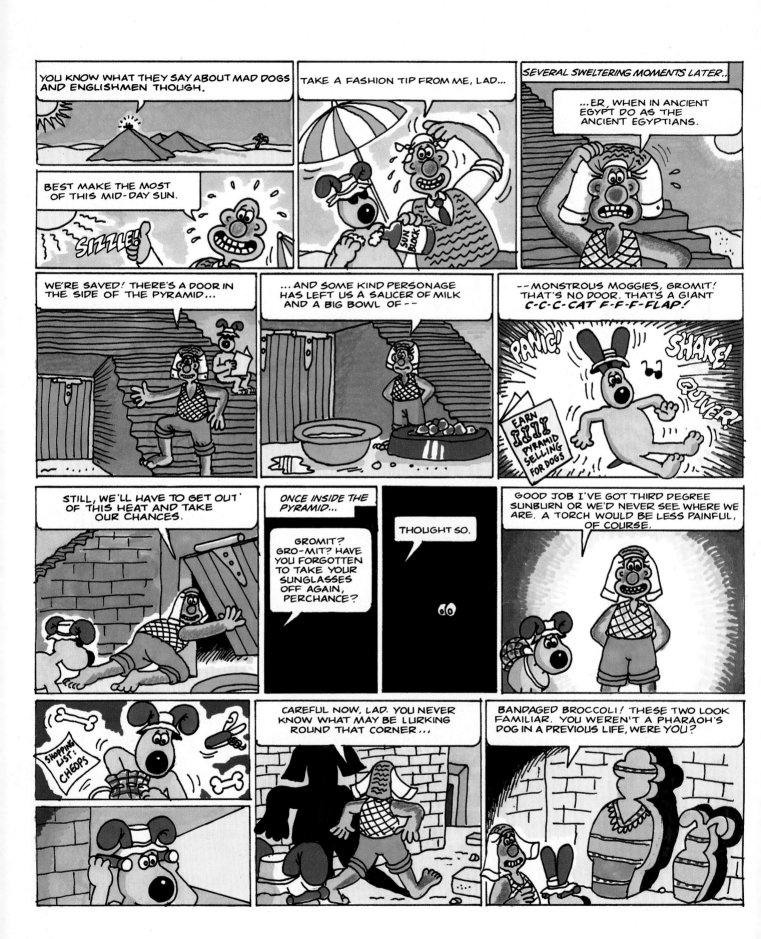

NO TIME FOR SNIFFING OTHER DOGS NOW, GROMIT. WE'VE GOT TO FIND MY SLIPPER.

SNIFF! TWITCH!

FOLLOW ME. WE MAY STUMBLE OVER ANOTHER...

C-L-U-E!!

AS I THOUGHT. THESE PYRAMIDS ARE FULL OF SECRET CHAMBERS WHERE A SHOE THIEF MIGHT BURY HIS TREASURES.

DON'T MIND THESE CHUMPS. THEY'RE ONLY STATUES TO SCARE OFF THE GULLIBLE.

BLINK!

SHIFTY STARE!

'COURSE IF THEY **WERE** REAL THEY COULD PROBABLY GIVE YOU A VERY NASTY NIP...

MY, WHAT HEAVY PAWS YOU HAVE ALL OF A SUDDEN, GROMIT.

TAP! TAP!

AND IF YOU DON'T MIND MY SAYING SO, IT'S TIME YOU CUT YOUR FINGERNAILS.

VERTIGINOUS VET'S BILLS!!! A M-M-MYTHOLOGICAL, EGYPTOLOGICAL...

... ORNITHOLOGICAL THINGUMMY. WITH LEGS. AND HE'S NOT ON A LEAD!!!

GRRRR

HE SEEMS TO BE TAKING US SOMEWHERE, GROMIT.

PERHAPS IT'S TO SEE HIS PHARAOH...

...AND IF WE DO MEET ROYALTY, WHATEVER YOU DO, DON'T FORGET TO BOW-WOW.

THE LANDING WAS BUMPY -- BUT AT LEAST WE DIDN'T BECOME THE IN-FLIGHT MEAL.

INSIDE THE PHARAOH'S PALACE...

THAT'S NEFER-TI-TI-TEA-FOR-TWO-TU-TANKHA -- THAT'S THE PHARAOH AND HIS MISSUS, THAT IS.

SORRY, LAD. THE ANCIENT EGYPTIANS WERE INCORRIGIBLE CAT FANCIERS, I'M AFRAID.

WE'D BETTER EXPLAIN WE WEREN'T ROBBING THE PYRAMID. I'LL DO A DRAWING. IT'S THE ONLY LANGUAGE THESE PEOPLE UNDERSTAND.

PARLEZ-VOUS HIEROGLYPHICS, ANY-ONE? WE'RE SLIPPER-HUNTERS FROM THE FUTURE!

I THINK PHARAOH'S GOT THE MESSAGE. AND NOW HE'S TELLING US ABOUT HIS FAMOUS PRISONS...

...AND, ER, HOW HE'S GOING TO LOCK US UP AND THROW AWAY THE KEY -- *HELP!!!*

CHIN UP, CHUCK. COULD BE WORSE. THEY MIGHT HAVE MADE US SLAVES AND HAD US WORKING LIKE, WELL, LIKE DOGS.

MOMENTS LATER...

EH, UP. SOMEONE'S COME TO TAKE YOU WALKIES.

ER, GROMIT WON'T BE NEEDING *TWO* COLLARS. HE'S GOT AN 'O' LEVEL IN OBEDIENCE.

JUST A MINUTE! THIS IS AGAINST THE GENEVA CONVENTION, THIS IS! YOU'LL BE HEARING FROM MY SOLICITOR!

ALL SMELLS VERY FISHY TO ME, LAD.

A TIN OPENER? WHERE ARE WE GOING WITH THAT?

NOUVELLE CUISINE! THEY'VE GOT US FEEDING THE PHARAOH'S CATS. THAT'S A DOG'S LIFE, THAT IS.

CHAMPION! THE CAT BURGLARS HAVE RETURNED AND THEIR BOOTY LOOKS DISTINCTLY SHOE-SHAPED.

WITH THEIR BUILT-IN 360-DEGREE VENTILATION SYSTEM, THESE OPEN-TOED SANDALS ARE PERFECT FOR EVEN THE HOTTEST OF --

FEVERISH PHARAOHS! HIS NIBS IS ON A WAR FOOTING.

IT APPEARS THAT SOMEONE'S FILCHED HIS FLIP-FLOPS.

HISSS! HISSS!

THERE'S GOING TO BE A PEN AND INK ABOUT THIS.

AS I FEARED. HE'S DRAWN THE WRONG CONCLUSION -- AND GUESS WHO'S FOR THE HIGH JUMP.

I WONDER IF WE'LL BE, ER HANGING AROUND HERE LONG ENOUGH TO APPEAL AGAINST OUR SENTENCE?

WE MIGHT HAVE A CAT'S CHANCE...

TUG! YANK! HEAVE!

... IF ONLY CATSHEBA CAN BEND THE PHARAOH'S EAR ...

... AND TAKE HIM TO WHERE YOU FOUND THE HOARD OF SANDALS.

GENEROUSLY, PHARAOH ALLOWS HIS PRISONERS TO CRAWL ACROSS THE DESERT IN THE MIDDAY SUN TO RETRIEVE HIS SMELLY OLD MISSING SHOES...

ONCE INSIDE THE PYRAMID...

REMINDS ME OF THE FILM 'BAREFOOT IN THE DARK' ACTUALLY.

THAT'S TORN IT. THE SHOE THIEF'S BEATEN US TO IT. NOW WE HAVEN'T A LEG TO STAND ON.

CHEESE

21

WE'VE BEEN VISITED BY TERRORIST TOPIARISTS -- OUR HEDGE WASN'T LIKE THAT WHEN WE LEFT.

BETTER FIND OUT WHAT YEAR IT IS...

EVENING SHOES
FOOTWEAR CRISIS LATEST!

NOW I'VE SEEN THE FORSEEABLE FUTURE -- AND IT'S HOPPING MAD!

THE SHOES 2096
COMPULSORY HOPPING TO BE MADE LAW!
INSOLE

THE SHOES 2096
CLOGS: THE HIDDEN MENACE!

OI! YOU TWO CAN'T STAND LIKE THAT! THAT'S BANNED, THAT IS. ONE LEG ONLY. PLANET CAN'T TAKE ANY MORE.

BOING!

BOING!

ANY MORE WHAT?

BOING!

BOING!

ANY MORE WEAR AND TEAR. NOT SINCE SOME PRIZE CHUMP, A VERITABLE BOBBY DAZZLER AMONG NINCOMPOOPS...

...INVENTED THE LONGLIFE INDOOR CARPET CLOG WITH REINFORCED EVERYTHING!

ER, LOOKS LIKE WE'VE PUT OUR FOOT IN IT.

THAT CLOG'S BEEN A MENACE-- A MENACE II SOCIETY!

BOING!

BOING!

IMPOSSIBLE! THEY'RE BIO-UN-DEGRADABLE.

THERE'S THE RUB: THE CLOGS NEVER WEAR OUT BUT EVERYTHING THEY TOUCH *DOES*.

LOOK WHAT HAPPENED TO CLOG-LOVING COUNTRIES WHERE THE TWO- OR THREE-CLOG FAMILY WAS THE NORM-- ENVIRONMENTAL DISASTER!

HOLLAND

EDAM NATION! WHAT'S THE ANTIDOTE?

HOP SWEET HOP

WELL, HOPPING'S KINDER TO THE PLANET BUT NOT TO SHOES: THEY WEAR OUT SO FAST THERE'S NOW A SHORTAGE. HENCE MY TIME-TRAVELLING 'BORROWINGS'.

BUT NOW I'M TRYING TO MASS PRODUCE THIS:

THIS! 'THIS' IS MY LOST SLIPPER, 'THIS' IS!

YOUR LOST SLIPPER? THEN YOU MUST BE GREAT-GREAT-GREAT UNCLE WALLACE, MAD INVENTOR EXTRAORDINAIRE.

A BIT LESS OF THE 'EXTRA-ORDINAIRE', IF YOU PLEASE. WHERE DID YOU FIND THESE SLIPPERY REMAINS?

SAME PLACE I FOUND THE DUSTY PLANS FOR YOUR GRANDFATHER CLOCK TIME MACHINE: STUFFED BEHIND THE RADIATOR WITH AN OLD BONE.

STUFFED BEHIND THE RADIATOR!!?? GROMIT!!! YOU'RE IN THE DOGHOUSE 'TIL WE SAVE CIVILIZATION FROM THIS HOPPING MAD SHOE SHORTAGE MULARKEY WE'VE CREATED.

FIRST THING IS TO RECREATE THE ORIGINAL COMFY CARPET SLIPPER. HOW'S THE PROTOTYPE?

CUSHIONED ARCH 'N' ANKLE SUPPORT, CHECK. TOE GRIP 'N' HEEL SWIVEL, CHECK. SOLE SLIDE 'N' BALL BOUNCE, CHECK. BUT IT'S STILL NOT COMFY.

DANGER! SLIPPER-TESTING IN PROGRESS

I'LL TELL YOU WHY NOT. IT'S THE WRONG COLOUR! GOT A POT OF RED, GREEN AND YELLOW PAINT, PERCHANCE?

AS EARTH CRACKS UNDER AEONS OF CLOG TRAFFIC... THE MET OFFICE ISSUED THE FOLLOWING WARNING ...

... PEDESTRIANS ARE ADVISED NOT TO APPROACH NORFOLK...

WHICH IS NOW COMPLETELY WORN OUT AND POTENTIALLY DANGEROUS...

TARTAN

CRIKEY! MUST GET THESE SLIPPERS FINISHED,...

... RECALL ALL OUR KILLER CARPET CLOGS AND REPLACE THE FOOT-WEAR YOU 'BORROWED' FROM THE TIME-SPACE CONTINUUM.

WONDER HOW THE TIME MACHINE REPAIRS ARE GOING?

BANG! BANG! BANG!

KEEP OUT DOGS AT WORK

FAN-SLIPPER-TASTIC, LADS! AND AN ONBOARD DIGITAL DISPLAY GIZMO TO BOOT!

WG 1

THE FUTURE IS ALL BEHIND US NOW AND THE PAST AHEAD -- LET OPERATION CLOG DAMAGE LIMITATION BEGIN!

WG 1

THE CURSE
OF THE
RAMSBOTTOMS

NIL DESPERANDUM, CHUCK!
(Which, along with *Per ardua ad Asda*, a traditional greeting at Roman supermarkets, is the only bit of Latin Wallace knows)

WALLACE
Inventor, handyman and gentleman motorcyclist, Wallace nurses a passion for the cheese of the Wensleydale region, and a tendresse for another local delicacy – the pulchritudinous Miss Wendolene Ramsbottom.

GROMIT
Bon viveur, bibliophile and barker, Wallace's constant travelling companion on the motorcycle is currently scripting a remake of Tennessee Williams' classic, *A Sidecar Named Desire*. Gromit's interest in bones remains undimmed, however. He is, after all, still a dog.

MISS WENDOLENE RAMSBOTTOM
Was there ever a maiden so fair as Wendolene, former wool shop proprietor and now the chatelaine of Ramsbottom Hall on 't' Ramsbottom Moor? Quite possibly there was – but not in this story there isn't.

PRESTON
Originally a cyber-dog created by Daddy, Wendolene's late father, Preston is undergoing modification as part of an ongoing series of improvements. Currently a cyber-butler powered by a rechargeable 12-volt car battery, everything is tickety-boo – except, that is, his voice control box which still suff. Ers. Tee. Thing. Probl. Ems. You get the pic. Ture.

RHETT LEICESTER
Charming, suave, debonair and sophisticated are just four of the flattering adjectives no-one in their right mind will ever apply to Rhett Leicester. An international cheese magnate, and Wendolene's lodger, Rhett's hobbies include garden gnomes and, er, garden gnomes.

BILL 'CHEESY' CHEESEMAN
* NOTE FROM THE PUBLISHERS: Due to circumstances beyond our control, no illustration is available of Mr Bill Cheeseman, Wensleydale's master cheesemaker. As you will read on the next page, he is currently missing on Ramsbottom Moor. We sincerely hope he turns up before the end of the story, and apologise for your temporary loss of picture.

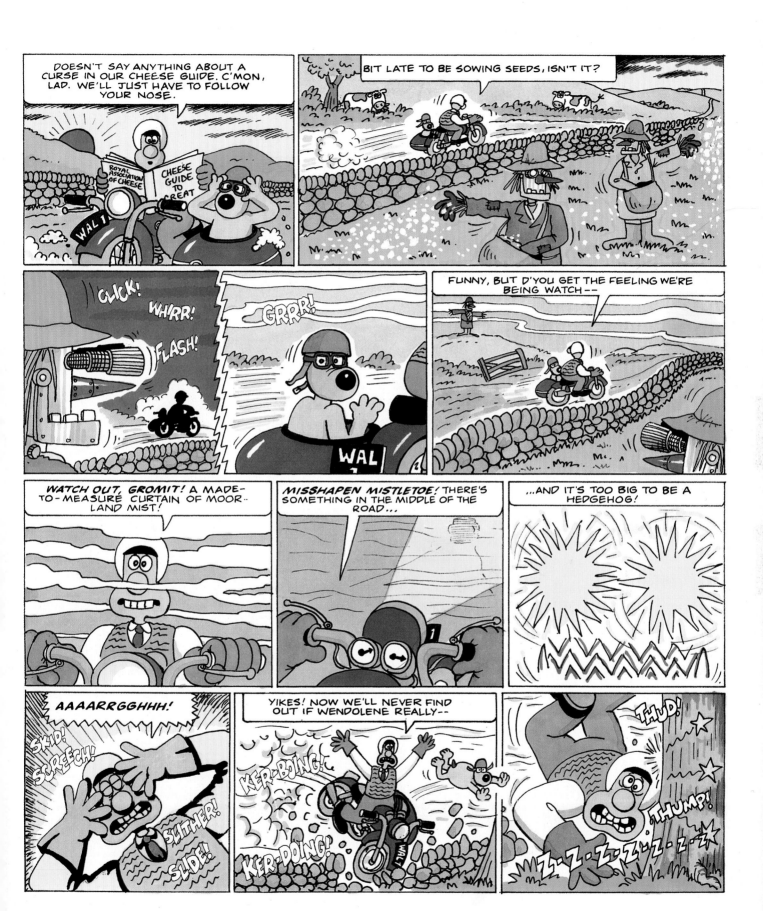

THE GUARDS'LL LET US IN. GOT TO BE A BIT CAREFUL ABOUT SECURITY. THEY SAY WE'RE CURSED UP HERE, YOU KNOW!

HEAVE! YANK! STRAIN!

VARROOM! VARROOM!

DIRTY RASCAL

ER, BIG PLACE YER UNCLE LEFT YOU! WHO DOES YER WINDOWS?

PRESTON. YOU REMEMBER PRESTON. HE'S BEEN IN FOR A SERVICE SINCE YOU LAST SAW HIM. HE'S NOW A CYBER-BUTLER.

ER, JUST YOU AND PRESTON UP 'ERE IS IT?

OH NO! COULDN'T LIVE UP 'ERE ON ME OWN. NO, THERE'S ALSO MY--

RHETT! RHETT LEICESTER!

Rhett Leicester CHEESE MAGNATE & LODGER

INTERNATIONAL CHEESE MAGNATE-- AND MS RAMSBOTTOM'S LODGER.

YOU MUST BE MR WALLACE. COME IN. WE'VE BEEN EXPECTING YOU!

LATER THAT EVENING...

SO WHAT BRINGS YOU TO RAMSBOTTOM MOOR?

THE CHEESE!

THE CHEESE?? THERE'S NO CHEESE ON RAMSBOTTOM MOOR!

SPLUTTER!

SEEMS I WAS MISINFORMED.

AHEM, GENTLEMEN. SHALL WE PARTAKE OF SOME LIGHT MUSICAL ACCOMPANIMENT?

... WE INTERRUPT THIS CONCERT BY THE WENSLEYDALE CHEESE ENSEMBLE TO BRING YOU A NEWS FLASH ...

... RESCUERS TONIGHT ABANDONED THEIR SEARCH FOR BILL 'CHEESY' CHEESEMAN, WENSLEYDALE'S MASTER CHEESEMAKER, FEARING HIM A VICTIM OF THE CURSE OF --

ER, WENDOLENE TELLS ME YOU DO A SPOT OF INVENTING. GNOMES ARE MY HOBBY. ORNAMENTAL GNOMES. IF YOU LIKE I CAN...

ELSEWHERE IN THE LIBRARY...

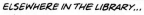

?!?

CHEESE MAKING FOR BEGINNERS

CURDS OF CURDISTAN

THE CURSE OF THE RAMSBOTTOMS

COLLECTED WORKS OF GNOME CHOMSKY

GRAB!

GRRR!

DINN. ER IS. SERV. ED.

GONG!

OUCH!

I HOPE YOU'RE FEELING PECKISH -- WE'RE HAVING CHEESE!

34

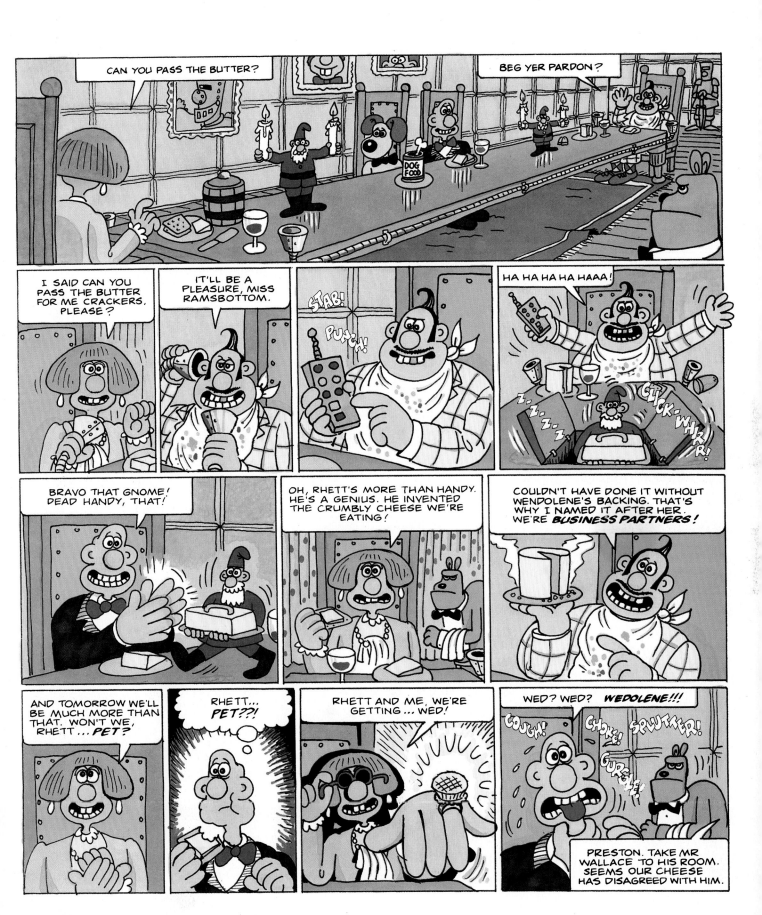

36

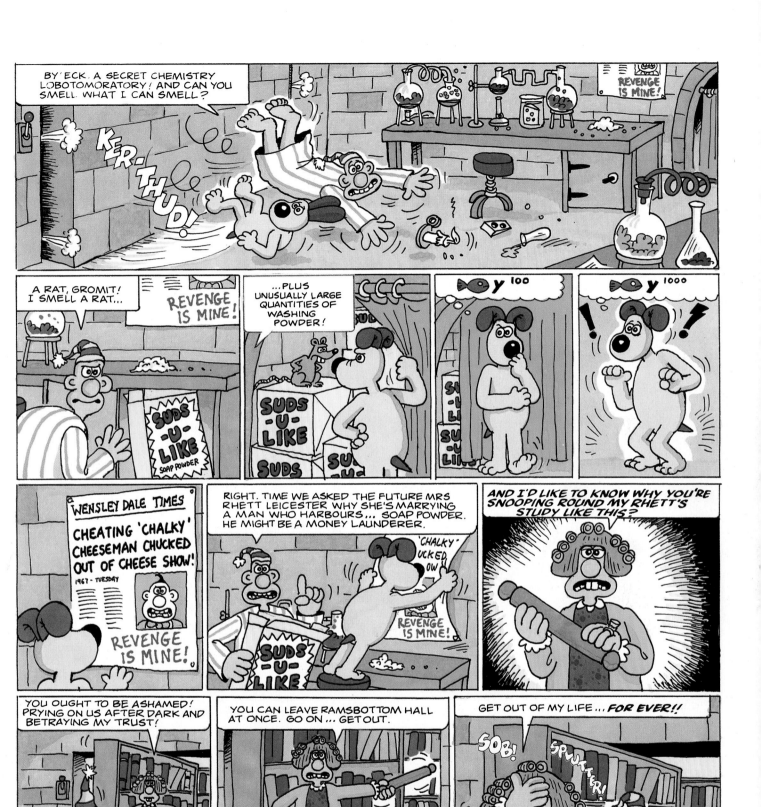

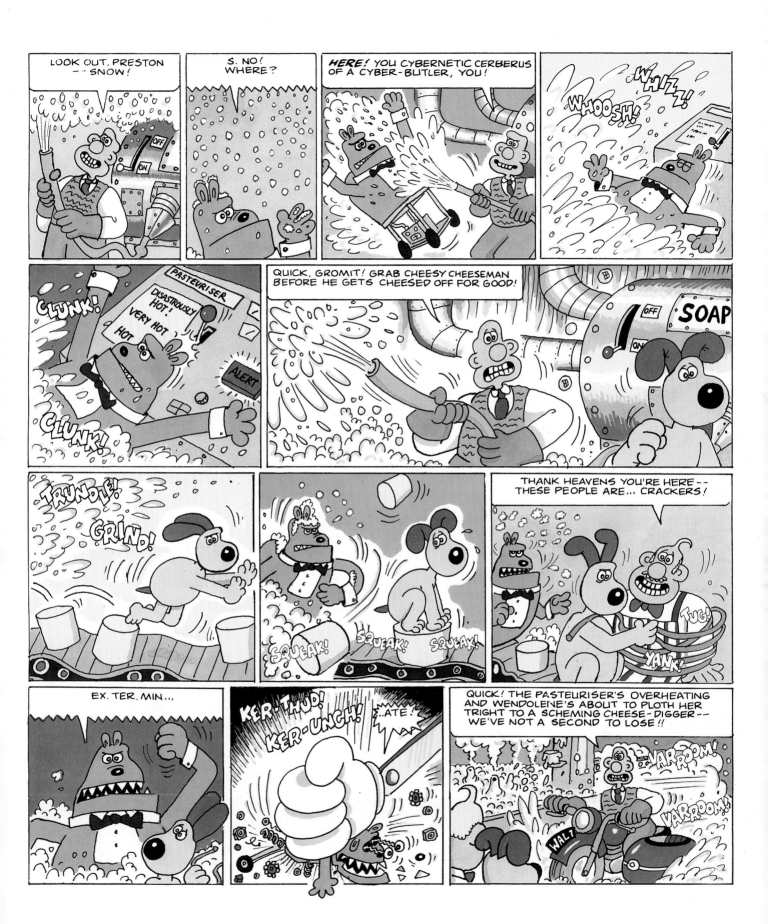

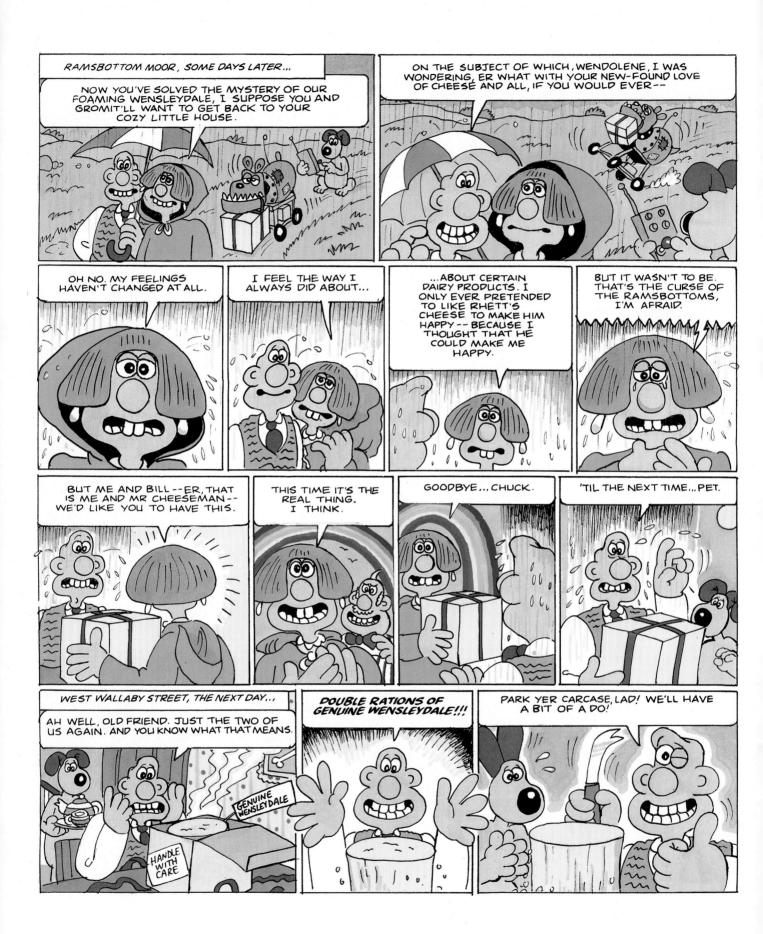

PRINTED IN BELGIUM BY proost INTERNATIONAL BOOK PRODUCTION